THE BEAST FROM CABIN X

BONEGARDEN #3

KARSTEN KNIGHT

The swamp was a terrible place to drive a convertible.

Yet here I was, speeding through the Louisiana bayou in the passenger seat of my dad's old Sebring. Tall cypress trees towered over the narrow road. Green swamp water the color of pea soup stretched for miles around us.

My father grinned at me from behind the steering wheel. "You smell that, Holly?" he asked. "That's the scent of adventure."

I wrinkled my nose. "Adventure smells a lot like rotting leaves," I replied.

The air conditioner had stopped working a hundred miles ago, leaving us with no choice but to lower the convertible's top. Even in the shade of the trees, the hot, humid air was suffocating.

I swatted at a swarm of gnats that flew right into my face. I must have been sweating pure sugar because the bugs here absolutely *adored* me.

I knew I shouldn't be complaining. After all, I was the reason we were driving through a swamp on the hottest day of summer.

Let me back up and explain:

For years, I had begged my dad to send me to sleep-away camp. Summer after summer, his response was always the same. "I'm sorry, Holly," he'd say. "It's just too expensive. Maybe next year."

Our budget had always been tight. As a single parent, my dad put in long hours at his mechanic shop just to make ends meet for us. My mom died when I was only a baby. I couldn't remember her face, but I wore a locket around my neck with her picture inside. My dad had given it to me when I was old enough to start asking questions about her.

I'd longed for the day when I would be able to attend camp and do all the things I read about in books—sleeping in a rustic cabin, swimming in a tranquil lake, telling ghost stories around a campfire. A girl could dream, couldn't she?

Then, last week, I came home to find my father

sitting on the sofa with a frown on his face. My suit-case rested on the coffee table in front of him. "I have some very bad news," he announced solemnly. He took a deep breath. "I have to send you away."

"What?" I choked out, panic rising in my chest. "W-what did I do wrong? Where are you sending me?"

Then I saw that he was struggling to keep from laughing. Unable to control himself any longer, he let out a high-pitched giggle. He was always playing pranks on me like this. "I have to send you away …" he repeated. This time he held up a pamphlet. "… for a summer at Camp Moonglow!"

I'm pretty sure the entire neighborhood heard my excited squeals.

Apparently, a spot at a camp in Louisiana had opened up at the last minute. "I told the director all about you and how camp has always been your dream," Dad explained. "He offered you a full schol-arship! The staff seemed eager to fill that last bed, so it's almost like you're doing *them* a favor."

At the time, it seemed too good to be true.

Now, as I sweated through my t-shirt, I started to wonder whether I'd made a big mistake. "I don't suppose the camp bunks are air-conditioned," I muttered.

My dad rolled his eyes. "It's a summer camp, not a five-star hotel," he replied. "Part of the experience is roughing it, living as one with nature. By the end of today, you'll be having so much fun that you won't even notice the heat."

I hoped he was right. "We must be getting close to Camp Moonglow by now," I said. Curious, I pulled the map out of the glove compartment and unfolded it. Our phones didn't get reception out in the bayou, so we had resorted to navigating the old-fashioned way.

As I squinted at the map, a shadow crossed in front of the sun. I looked up—

—just in time to see the massive cypress tree falling across the road.

With a mighty groan, its roots tore right out of the soggy ground. The trunk slammed down directly in front of the car.

"Dad, watch out!" I screamed. Then I braced for impact.

D ad slammed on the brakes and jerked the steering wheel hard to the left. The car fishtailed sideways over the asphalt.

Miraculously, we came to a hard stop just inches from the mighty tree trunk. My face was so close to the wood I could make out the elaborate pattern of its bark.

It took me a few seconds to realize I was screaming. I forced myself to stop and took a few deep breaths.

"You okay?" my dad asked, examining me over the armrest. "Anything broken?"

I massaged my throat. "Just my vocal cords," I replied. "And my dignity."

I stumbled out of the car. The smell of burning

rubber wafted off the pavement. I followed the trail of brake marks the tires left on the road.

My dad rubbed the back of his neck and frowned at the cypress blocking our path. "I thought trees were supposed to yell 'Timber!' before they fell," he said.

Even in near-death situations, my father cracked jokes.

"Y'all okay?" a voice asked from behind us.

I spun around. A teenage girl had appeared beside the fallen tree. Every piece of her outfit was the same pea-soup green of the swamp, from her polo shirt and tennis shorts to the knee-high socks and her sneakers. She'd threaded her blonde ponytail through the back of a baseball cap.

"We're, uh, fine," my dad finally answered for us. "I can't say the same for this tree, though."

The girl tapped the trunk with her foot. "At least we'll have some new kindling to burn at the camp bonfire tonight," she said. Her voice had a southern twang.

My eyes lit up. "Wait, you're from Camp Moonglow?" I asked.

"Guilty as charged. I'm Laurel, the head counselor." She looked back and forth between me and my father. "Which one of you is my new camper?"

"I'm Holly," I said, shaking her hand. "How did you find us?"

"Wasn't hard," she replied. "Just followed the screech of brakes and the sound of someone screaming. Pretty sure they could hear you all the way back in Mississippi."

I blushed. Seeing that I was embarrassed, my dad cleared his throat. "The screaming was me. Holly here is the brave one." He pointed to the fallen tree. "Looks like our only way onward is blocked, and I think the bayou will swallow my convertible whole if we try to drive around this. Any chance you can lead us back to camp?"

I was surprised when Holly shook her head. "No, I'm afraid I can't do that," she said, then added menacingly, "*The two of you ain't going anywhere.*"

3

"What?" My voice came out shriller than I wanted. We'd come so far driving through this hot, smelly swamp. Now, this crazy counselor intended to just leave us stranded in the middle of nowhere?

A wicked grin broke across her face. "I can't lead you to the camp," she continued, "because you're already here!"

Laurel gestured with her arm toward the other side of the fallen tree. I moved until the trunk was no longer blocking my view of the road.

Just ahead, I spotted an old wooden sign carved in the shape of a gator. In messy white painted letters, it read: "Welcome to Camp Moonglow." Beyond it, a path snaked through the trees.

My dad burst into laughter. "You should have seen the look on your face!" he said. "At least the counselors here have the same great sense of humor as me. You'll never get homesick!"

"Lucky me," I muttered. Maybe the camp offered a class that would teach me to be less gullible.

Laurel waved a hand, gesturing for us to follow her. "Come on now. I'll give y'all the official tour."

After a short walk down the path, we approached a series of dark wooden cabins. Another counselor dressed in the same green uniform led a group of campers past us. None of the girls seemed to be having a great time.

I took a closer look at the cabins where everyone slept. They didn't at all resemble the clean, picturesque cottages from the pictures in the brochure. No, these bunks looked like someone had hastily slapped them together using rotting wooden planks and rusty nails. The bayou waters crept right up to their foundations, threatening to swallow them up.

"Beautiful craftsmanship, isn't it?" Laurel asked, her voice full of admiration.

I started to laugh—then stifled it when I realized she wasn't kidding.

The cafeteria wasn't in much better shape.

Campers crowded around long tables, eating a brown soup I couldn't immediately identify.

"This is where you'll eat most of your meals," Laurel explained. "Chef Heather is one of the finest cooks in Alameda County."

Aside from the triangular roof, it was open to the bayou air. An army of flies swarmed around the inside, diving in for bites of the soup while campers slapped them away.

I tried to find a bright side in all of this. So what if the bunks and the cafeteria needed some repairs. My dad was right—I didn't go to camp just to spend my summer inside. "What about the lake?" I asked. "I'm excited to practice my swimming this summer."

"Aha!" Laurel cried. "Then you've come to the right place."

She led us over to a long dock that extended into the bayou. At the end of the pier, she gestured out at the swamplands beyond. "Ta-da!" she said.

I stared in confusion out at the same green bayou waters we'd be driving through for an hour. The only difference was that the water in this area seemed deeper.

The front page of the camp brochure had promised a crystal-clear lake, with campers diving off the docks, while the sun set dramatically behind them.

"You guys swim in this?" I asked, my voice incredulous.

"Every single day!" Laurel replied. She poked at a rope swing dangling from the tree above us. "The beauty of living in the bayou is that everywhere you look is an opportunity to swim."

I stared down into the muck. It was impossible to tell what lurked beneath the surface. "What about gators?" I asked.

Laurel waved a hand dismissively. "They don't mind sharing their swimming hole."

I looked to my dad, trying to gauge his reaction. I could see that he was skeptical as well. He knelt in front of me. "What do you think, sport?" He studied my face. I could tell that all I had to do was say the word and he'd take us home. We'd march right back to the car and make a U-turn.

But then I realized how ungrateful I was being. I'd spent years pleading with him to send me to camp, and he'd found a way to make it happen.

Maybe Camp Moonglow wasn't exactly the paradise the brochure had promised. However, if I went home now, I'd live the same repetitive, boring summer that I always did, biking the same loop around my hometown.

I forced a smile. "I think it's going to be a great summer."

He gave me a fist-bump. "That's the spirit," he said. "I have a feeling that by the end of the summer, I'm going to have to *drag* you out of the bayou."

Looking back on it, he should have chosen his words more carefully.

4

After the tour was over, we trekked back to the convertible. Laurel unloaded my duffle bag while I hugged my father goodbye.

"I don't think your cell phone will be much use out here, but the camp director should have a land-line in his office if you need to reach me," he said. "And I saw on the weekly schedule that they let you write letters to send home—I better get at least one!"

I hugged him back. "I'm sure I can squeeze a letter or two into my busy schedule," I replied.

Minutes later, I waved as the convertible vanished around the corner. Laurel stepped up beside me, my duffle bag slung across her back. She grimaced under the weight of it. "What did you pack in here, your cannonball collection?" she asked. "Come on, it's time to meet your bunkmates."

I felt nervous as she escorted me to Cabin IX, my home for the next two months. All of the other campers had been here for a few weeks, which meant they'd had extra time to make new friends. What if they treated me like an outsider for showing up so late?

Here goes nothing, I thought as we arrived outside the ramshackle cabin. Laurel turned the handle and pushed open the warped door.

I stepped into the dimly lit bunk. The floorboards creaked under my feet.

The cabin was so cramped that the two bunk beds filled most of the space. Two girls were playing a dice game on the floor. Like me, they must have been about twelve years old. Two piles of chocolate bars sat between them. It looked like they were betting with them.

A third girl, smaller than the others, was curled up in one of the bunks. She had her faced buried in a book and showed no interest in the game the others were playing.

One of the campers on the floor rolled two sixes on the dice and jumped to her feet. She released a cry of victory and thumped her fist against her chest.

"Finally, I have defeated you!" she proclaimed. "Take that, you cheating—"

She abruptly shut up when she noticed Laurel and me. The other girl smoothly brushed her pile of chocolate under the bed.

Laurel cleared her throat. "Darcy, Stella, Camille," she said. "I want to introduce you to your new bunkmate, Holly."

Darcy, the girl who had won the game, stepped forward to shake my hand. She wore a wide-brimmed fedora and a khaki outfit. She instantly reminded me of a fearless explorer, or maybe the star of one of those television shows where they handle wild animals. "Welcome to Camp Moonglow," she said. Her handshake was so enthusiastic I thought my arm might snap right off.

Stella was extremely pale with dark, short-cropped hair. I couldn't decide whether she looked like a fashion model or a vampire. It was hard to imagine her traipsing about the swamp in her combat boots.

When I looked closer, I saw that her shirt was handmade out of electrical tape and scraps of old band t-shirts. She noticed me admiring it and grinned. "I design my own clothes. I can make you one just like it," she offered.

Darcy nodded to the reading girl. "The bookworm is Camille," she said. "She only ever comes down to find a new book or to feed."

"What are you reading?" I asked her.

Camille finally looked up from her book, offering me a shy smile. "It's a guide on local legends about ghosts and monsters in the bayou," she explained. "You'd be surprised how many weird and unexplained phenomena happen around here."

Even in the sweltering heat of the cabin, I couldn't help but shiver. "I'm sure you're right," I replied.

Before Laurel left us, she announced that there was a cookout planned for later that evening. I decided I better start unpacking. Each of us had a small trunk where we could store our things.

Darcy pointed to one of the top bunks. "That bed is yours, right above mine," she said. "I don't mind switching with you if you'd rather not climb."

I smiled. "No, the top bunk will do just fine. I'm just happy a bed opened up at the last minute."

Instantly, I could tell that I'd said the wrong thing. Darcy and Stella exchanged suspicious glances. Even Camille's eyes widened above her book.

Curiosity got the better of me. "Where did the previous camper go, anyway?" I asked. "Did she decide she couldn't stand the mosquitoes any longer?"

For a moment, no one responded. Then Darcy glanced over at the door as if to make sure no one else was listening. "We don't know," she whispered. "One day the girl who slept in that bunk just vanished out of thin air."

5

"Vanished?" I repeated. Darcy had to be kidding, right? I glanced between my bunkmates' faces but they all looked dead serious. "Where could she possibly go? There's only bayou for miles around."

Stella shook her head. "It makes no sense," she said. "No one knows why Rachel left—she loved this camp more than anyone. She'd been coming here since the first grade. She was always off exploring the bayou and never complained once about the heat."

"Heck, she even liked the *food*," Darcy added, pinching her nose closed. "All we know is that one night, she never showed up for the campfire. When we got back to the cabin, her bed was neatly made and her belongings were gone. No goodbye, no note —it was like she was never here at all."

A chill coursed through me. "Maybe her family had an emergency," I suggested. "Maybe she had to leave so quickly that she didn't have a chance to say goodbye."

Stella shrugged. "Maybe. Maybe not. When we asked Laurel, she told us to mind our own business. We even tried to go right to the camp director, but he never comes out of his office and it was locked when we tried the door."

I didn't like the sound of any of this. A missing camper. Counselors who evaded questions. A director who didn't care that a couple of teenagers were running the camp.

My thoughts were interrupted by a horn blowing somewhere in the distance. "That's the call to dinner," Darcy explained. "We better get moving."

Dinner already? I thought. I'd just seen half the camp eating that slop in the cafeteria.

Stella poked Camille. "You sure you don't want to come with us?" she asked the reading girl. "They're serving burgers and veggie dogs tonight—for once it's not something that includes the word 'gumbo.'"

"No thanks," Camille said. "I just really need—"

"—to finish this chapter," Darcy and Stella

intoned in unison. They'd clearly heard that excuse before.

The girls led me on a different route through camp than Laurel had. "The unofficial tour," they called it. They showed me an old ropes course high up in the trees, and an archery range with arrows scattered around the bulls-eyes.

Along the way, I spied a dark structure hidden in the brush. "What is *that?*" I asked. Before the others had a chance to explain, I moved off the path to get a closer look.

At one point it had been a cabin just like ours.

Only something had destroyed this one.

The walls were charred black. The roof had burned away, leaving the interior open to the weather. Glass shards littered the leaves around it where the windows had been smashed to bits.

A copper "X" hung over the doorway, green with rust.

Stella and Darcy lingered behind me. "That's Cabin X," Stella said in a hushed voice. "There used to be ten bunks when they built the camp. Then, last summer, something horrible happened in this one."

"What do you mean 'something horrible?'" I asked. I found myself whispering, too.

Darcy tightly gripped her fedora. "No one knows

for sure," she replied. "But I've heard rumors. Some campers claim that the girls living here performed an ancient ritual. They didn't think anything would come of it. They were wrong."

"In the middle of the ritual, a lightning bolt forked down from the sky," Stella continued. "It punched a hole right through the roof and set Cabin X ablaze. When the counselors saw the flames, they tried to extinguish it using buckets of swamp water. But they were too late."

"Everyone inside had been reduced to ashes," Darcy finished.

Somewhere inside the charred cabin, I heard a rustling sound. "Wait," I whispered. "Do you hear that?"

It grew louder.

Then, with a tremendous *BANG*, the trespasser inside pounded against the door.

6

D arcy, Stella, and I all screamed in unison. Something pounded the door again. The blackened wood rattled on its hinges.

Then silence.

We stood frozen to the spot, unsure whether to run. Any moment now, the door might swing open and whatever was inside would come chasing after us.

Then a dark figure pounced up into the broken window.

It was just a raccoon. The furry creature perched on the sill, its beady eyes studying us with curiosity. It finally hopped down and scampered off into the trees.

After a tense moment, we all burst into laughter. I

was glad I wasn't the only one who had been spooked.

Once our heart rates slowed to normal, I followed the girls down the rest of the path. It eventually opened up into a small clearing full of campers. A large bonfire roared at its center. Old logs had been laid out around it as seats.

We must have been the last to arrive, thanks to our scenic detour past Cabin X. The three of us wandered over to the buffet line. The counselors were struggling to cook burgers and hotdogs as fast as the campers were eating them. I spotted Laurel mixing a vat of potato salad with a big spoon.

Once everyone had food, we sat down by the bonfire. I met a few girls from other bunks who seemed nice. For the first time, Camp Moonglow was starting to feel like the summer camps I'd always read about.

As the sun set, I looked up into the canopy of trees. Dark shapes darted overhead—bats, I realized. Lots and lots of bats.

A pile of bat droppings landed on one camper's hamburger. She shrieked and chucked the whole thing into the fire, while the rest of us roared with laughter.

Eventually, Laurel stepped up onto a big rock

near the bonfire so everyone could see her. She raised her hands over her head and made a hooting sound like an owl. The girls around me all began to hoot back at her, even Stella and Darcy. I joined in so I wouldn't look like an outsider. It must have been the camp signal for everyone to pay attention.

With everyone's focus on her, Laurel gazed around at the campers. The firelight flickered over her face. "Since all of you are going to be here for an entire summer, it seems only fair to tell you about some … unexplained things that have happened in the bayou. *Terrible* things."

Darcy rubbed her hands together. "Ooh, I love a good ghost story," she whispered to me.

Laurel's head snapped around and she narrowed her eyes at Darcy. "This is not some made-up ghost story," she corrected her. "This is a cautionary tale about the dangers that lurk in the shadows."

Darcy had spoken so quietly—how had Laurel possibly overheard her?

Laurel stared pensively off into the woods. "There are many, many legends about the bayou," she went on. "Humans have lived in this region for thousands of years, and they've reported seeing all sorts of strange things. Lights in the treetops that can't be explained. Spirits haunting those who dare to trespass over their watery graves. But perhaps no beast was more feared in these parts …" Laurel turned on a flashlight and illuminated her face from below. "… than the Rougarou."

The Rougarou? I thought. It sounded more like a soup than a scary creature.

She shined her flashlight around the group as she continued. "Over two hundred years ago, a group of people known as the Acadians traveled all the way down from Canada to settle here. This camp is built on the site of one of their very first towns. They constructed cabins for their families to live in and ate crawfish they caught in the water. At first, the bayou seemed like a safe, peaceful place to settle down. If only they knew what waited for them in the shadows …"

A chill coursed through me. *It's just a story intended to scare us,* I reminded myself. *Don't be a chicken on your first day of camp.*

Standing in front of the crackling flames, Laurel looked demonic as the story continued. "It started when people noticed claw marks on the trees around town. Deep ones, big ones, made by a large animal. At night, when the moon was full, they could hear something howling in the woods. Then livestock began to go missing. Sheep and chickens would disappear from their pens. Days later, they'd find the carcasses deep in the swamp. It looked like an animal had torn them to shreds."

Stella, who had been about to bite into her third hamburger, dropped it back onto her plate. "Well, there goes my appetite," she grumbled.

"The settlers thought it must be a coyote or a wolf," Laurel continued. "So a few hunters from the village decided to track the creature down. Three of them set out into the bayou. By the next morning, *only one returned alive.*"

I gazed around the circle. Some of the older campers giggled, not taking the story seriously. The younger ones looked terrified, clutching each other in fear.

"The lone survivor told a terrifying story. After the hunters had left camp, they sensed that something was following them, stalking them through the swamp. Night fell and they became lost. One of the hunters set out to find wood for a fire. When he didn't return, the other two went looking for him—until they stopped dead in their tracks. In their path, they saw a large, dog-like creature on its haunches feeding on the body of the missing hunter."

Laurel crouched low on the rock, pretending to be the animal. "Then the creature saw them. It rose up onto its hind legs." She straightened up, stretching taller. "Even though it had the head of a wolf, it could walk on two legs like a human."

At this, somebody on the other side of the circle groaned. "Wait, so this story is about a werewolf?"

Laurel shook her head. "Oh, no. The Rougarou is so much worse than a werewolf. This one was nearly ten feet tall. It had three rows of razor-sharp teeth. Its eyes glowed yellow. A werewolf only turns into a beast at the full moon, but the Rougarou can transform whenever it likes. The werewolf hunts because it has to. The Rougarou hunts because it *likes* to."

As she went on, Laurel's voice grew excited. "The two men turned and ran as the beast loped after them. They could hear its hungry snarls as it got closer and closer. One of the fleeing hunters was slower than the other and the Rougarou tackled him to the ground. The last remaining hunter listened to his friend's screams as he raced back to the village."

Laurel took a deep breath. She suddenly looked tired from telling the story. "To this day, people still swear they hear the Rougarou's howls echo through the bayou. And if you should ever be so unfortunate as to cross paths with one …" Her gaze landed on me. "… Then you better hope that you're not the slowest runner in your bunk."

I heard the crunch of leaves behind me too late. Heavy footsteps thumped toward me.

Before I had the chance to turn around, a hand clamped down on my shoulder.

I let out a shrill scream as I saw the coat of wolf's fur covering the fingers.

7

The werewolf's claws tightened on my shoulder. I struggled to free myself. When I finally shrugged out of its grip, I slipped off the log and fell back-first onto the muddy ground.

That's when I saw that the wolf's claw was attached to a very human-looking counselor with short spiky hair. She grinned down at me.

The claw was just part of a costume.

All around the fire, the campers burst into laughter. My cheeks burned red with embarrassment. How could I have fallen for such a stupid prank?

The counselor, Tonya, bent over and held out the wolf's claw. It took me a moment to realize she was offering to help me up.

"Sorry, I didn't mean to scare you *that* bad," she said as she pulled me to my feet.

I tried to brush the mud off my shorts as I reclaimed my seat on the log. Stella patted me on the back. "Don't sweat it," she whispered reassuringly. "The counselors have been doing this since day one."

Darcy shook her head and added, "If you ask me, I think they get a little too much enjoyment out of terrifying us."

I locked eyes with Laurel. In the firelight, the grin on her face looked downright sinister.

I DIDN'T SLEEP well my first night at camp. For hours, I found myself tossing and turning. Maybe it was just the unfamiliar bed, with its scratchy sheets and lumpy mattress. Maybe it was all the sounds, from Stella's snoring to the croak of bullfrogs outside.

The terrifying story of the Rougarou didn't help either.

Every time I closed my eyes, I felt that hairy hand squeezing my shoulder. The bayou was creepy enough already—why were the counselors so obsessed with scaring the campers?

Eventually, I must have fallen asleep because I

awoke to two hands shaking me. I was so disoriented that for a moment I thought I was back home, sleeping in my own bed.

When the shaking persisted, I opened one tired eye. Laurel peered at me from between the bunk slats. "Rise and shine, sleepyhead," she announced in a chipper voice.

I sat up slowly, stretching my sore muscles. "What time is it?" I asked, glancing out the window. The sun had barely begun to rise. "Never mind, I don't want to know."

Laurel tossed me a pair of shorts from my open suitcase. "Since you're a new arrival, I went ahead and signed you up for activities this week," she explained. "That way you can get a taste of everything Camp Moonglow has to offer."

This cheered me up a little. The daily activities were what made sleeping in a hot, humid bunk worth it for campers like me, right? "What am I signed up for this morning?" I asked.

Laurel handed me an itinerary. The first item simply read "Fishing" in sloppily written marker, with no further explanation.

"Be at the docks in fifteen minutes," Laurel called back to me as she disappeared out the front door before I could ask more questions.

I was relieved when Darcy said she'd signed up for the fishing trip as well. After we dressed, I followed her across camp. This time, I suppressed a shudder as we passed the charred ruins of Cabin X.

At the edge of camp, Darcy and I found a small group of other campers waiting on a wooden pier. The bayou didn't seem particularly deep so I wondered what kind of boat could navigate these waters without running aground.

My question was soon answered when I heard a low hum. The noise grew louder until a strange boat appeared in the distance. It had a low, flat hull that skipped over the water like a stone. A giant fan attached to the back propelled it forward.

I recognized the spiky-haired counselor piloting the boat: Tonya, the one who had scared me half to death with the wolf hand.

I hoped she'd left her scary movie props back on the mainland today.

We all climbed into the rigid fiberglass hull. I was the last to board, and before I could even sit down, Tonya pushed the throttle forward. The boat lurched away from the pier and I toppled back into my seat.

The propeller's giant blades whirred loudly behind us as we sped through the bayou. I gripped the side for dear life as Tonya threaded the boat between the trees. The wind rushing past us was so intense I thought it was going to blow the elastic right out of my ponytail.

Darcy lowered a pair of flight goggles over her eyes. "I don't even like fishing!" she yelled over the raging wind. "I just signed up for the ride!"

I barely heard her last few words. As we sailed past a tree, I spotted something that made my blood run cold.

Five giant claw marks slashed into the bark.

8

A s we got closer, I saw even more claw marks crisscrossing the trunk. It looked like an animal had gone bonkers trying to tear apart the tree.

Whatever creature had done this had been massive.

I pointed with a trembling finger at the trunk. "W-what kind of animal did that?" I asked.

"Probably a woodpecker," Darcy suggested. "You can hear them hacking away at the trees all day long."

"You think a *beak* made those lines?" I said incredulously.

Darcy shrugged. "I guess it could have been a coyote."

The claw marks were over my head. "Unless the coyote was wearing stilts …" I started to say.

My train of thought was interrupted as Tonya let off the throttle. We coasted to a stop in a section of bayou that looked no different from all the others— just murky water and towering cypress trees.

I glanced around the boat, suddenly realizing something. "Hey, where are the fishing rods?" I asked Tonya. Aside from us campers, the only object in the boat was an empty metal tub. "Are we supposed to catch the fish with our bare hands?"

The counselor stared blankly at me, eyes hidden behind a pair of reflective sunglasses. She was chewing on a piece of grass. "Not that kind of fishin'," she responded curtly. "I reckon you'll find this much more fun."

"I think the new girl should go first," one of the campers suggested. She sneered at me, and it was only then I realized that I was the "new girl" she meant.

I expected Tonya to stick up for me. Instead, a mischievous grin slithered across her face. "That's a great idea," she replied. "The best way to learn is by diving right in."

Tonya pointed to a patch of water thirty feet from

the boat. I couldn't see at first, so I stepped up onto the edge to get a closer look. Squinting through the morning light, I spotted a white plastic object floating on the surface. A buoy, I recognized as I peered closer.

"You ... want me to swim over there?" I asked uncertainly, staring down into the cloudy, green water.

Tonya shrugged. "The fish aren't going to catch themselves, are they?"

I turned to protest, to ask her to steer the boat closer—but then I stepped on a slippery patch. My feet flew out from beneath me and I flailed helplessly to regain my balance.

With a shriek, I slipped right off the boat and hit the water hard.

I plunged beneath the surface. For a moment I couldn't figure out which way was up and which way was down.

When I finally resurfaced, I heard laughter. All of the other campers must have thought my fall was hilarious.

At least Darcy was nice enough to look concerned. She leaned over the edge of the boat to see if I was okay.

I waved her off, trying to make it look like the fall

was no big deal. I spat a few times to clear the swamp water out of my mouth. It tasted like old leaves and algae. I couldn't even imagine how I would smell by the time I returned to camp.

With relief, I discovered that the shallow water only came up to my waist. I waded toward the buoy, trying to move as quickly as possible. The sooner I got out of the water, the better. Beneath my sandals, the bottom of the bayou wriggled as though it were alive. I couldn't see what I was stepping on through the murky water.

Finally, I reached the buoy. "What now?" I called back to the boat.

"There's a line tied to the bottom," Tonya yelled back. "Follow it until you feel the metal trap."

Metal trap? I wondered. What kind of fish were they catching out here?

After groping around beneath the buoy, I found the line Tonya was talking about. I grabbed ahold of it and followed it through the water.

I had traveled maybe ten feet when my toe struck something hard. The line was tied to a metal object beneath the surface. I cautiously dipped my hands lower, lower, until my face touched the water.

The surface of the object had a lot of holes in it, like a cheese grater. It was shaped like a cylinder.

Cautiously, I gripped the trap on both sides and lifted. It was heavier than I expected—maybe it had successfully trapped a fish.

The moment it broke the surface, I let out a piercing scream when I saw what was inside.

9

Small red creatures filled the metal container. There must have been more than a hundred of them, crawling over each other. They had dark, crimson exoskeletons, two sharp claws, and too many spindly legs to count. Antennae wiggled on their ugly little heads.

They looked like lobsters but much smaller.

"What's the matter, Holly?" Tonya called out to me. "Never seen a crawdaddy before?"

I'd read about these creatures in a travel book on Louisiana. Crawfish—or crawdaddies as they were sometimes called—lived in the freshwater rivers and bayous here. People would boil and eat them in a variety of different local dishes. Most of the world's crawfish were caught right here in Louisiana.

Even if they tasted good, it didn't make holding a big metal trap crawling with them any less disgusting.

Still, I didn't want to look like a coward. I'd been embarrassed enough over the last twenty-four hours.

So I hoisted the heavy trap on my shoulder and waded back over to the boat. Tonya took the trap out of my hands, and Darcy helped pull me back up into the boat.

Tonya dumped the nimble little creatures into the giant tub. When she was done, she narrowed her eyes at the other campers. "What are y'all waiting for?" She pointed to all the buoys out in the swamp. "Get to work."

We must have been out there for nearly an hour. Tonya didn't let us stop until the crawfish filled the metal vat to the brim. As Darcy and I worked together, I said, "This is kind of weird, don't you think?"

"What do you mean?" Darcy asked between grunts as we lifted a heavy trap out of the water.

I glanced back at the boat to make sure we were out of earshot. "This feels more like slave labor than a camp activity," I whispered.

Darcy nodded thoughtfully. "I heard another girl complain about the same thing last week. Tonya snapped at her—she said if we wanted to eat the dining hall food, it was our responsibility to help catch it."

I frowned. "I … guess that makes sense."

"There's just one problem with that explanation," Darcy replied, lowering her voice. "They've *never* served crawfish in the dining hall."

That was weird. Were the counselors hoarding all the good food? Were they selling the crawfish on the side for extra money?

I noticed Tonya scowling in our direction, so I stopped asking questions.

However, I vowed to find out what was going on here, one way or another.

By the time Tonya called us all back to the boat, my clothes and hair were completely soaked with a mixture of sweat and swamp water. As we sped back toward camp, I pulled the soggy paper itinerary that Laurel had given me out of my pocket. According to the agenda, my afternoon activity involved "the ropes course."

As I watched the crawfish in the vat scuttle all over each other, I felt grateful that fishing was the only activity on today's itinerary that included icky swamp creatures.

I wish I'd known then that my encounters with the beasts of the bayou were only just beginning.

And they were about to get a whole lot more frightening.

When I arrived at the ropes course, I was relieved to see my other bunkmates, Stella and Camille, among the campers. Stella had dressed in camouflage exercise clothes she'd designed herself. It looked like she was about to go to war.

Meanwhile, Camille was lounging in a hammock with her nose buried in yet another old book. On closer inspection, I realized the hammock was just one of the bedsheets from our bunk that she'd tied between two trees. I imagined the counselors had dragged her out of the cabin against her will.

I craned my neck to look up at the course, a series of ropes that formed a giant web between the trees. Some of them must have been thirty feet above the ground. You had to climb a ladder to reach any of it.

"We're supposed to walk across those?" I asked, my voice squeakier than I intended. "All the way up there? That can't possibly be safe."

"It's perfectly safe," promised a voice behind me —Laurel. I hadn't even heard her approach. It was as if she had materialized out of thin air. She offered me a hollow smile as she walked away. "No one has died yet this year."

"What do you mean *yet*?" I asked, then added. "And what do you mean *this year*?!"

Beside me, Stella did a series of stretches. "Don't let her scare you," she said. "For the higher ropes, they put you in a safety harness. If you slip off, you'll just safely glide to the ground. Isn't that right, Camille?"

Camille laughed but didn't look up from the guidebook on alligators she was reading. "Oh, I don't actually participate," she explained. "I just find it entertaining hearing everyone's screams when they fall."

I swallowed hard.

Laurel climbed onto a stump and clapped her hands together. "Okay, Camp Moonglow. Who is going to be our first victim today? Any volunteers?" Her gaze slowly drifted over the campers …

… Then settled directly on me.

What was up with these counselors? I wondered. Why were they so fixated on singling me out? Did they do this to every camper unfortunate enough to be labeled "the new girl?"

I could see her opening her mouth to call on me, so I decided to beat her to the punch. "I'll do it," I offered. Maybe a display of courage would get the counselors to give me a break.

Laurel studied me. "Thank you, Holly," she replied finally. "Since this is your first time, I think I'll have you start with the Slurry."

"*The Slurry?*" I repeated. It sounded more like an ice cream sundae than an obstacle course.

"Yes," she said with a mischievous grin. "Of all the courses, it's the lowest to the ground."

I quickly found out that Laurel hadn't done me any favors. She led me over to a rope bridge that, true to her word, was low to the ground.

Because it stretched out over a gigantic sinkhole.

The crater looked like a giant had punched a hole right in the middle of the bayou. It was impossible to tell how deep it went because of the water at the bottom.

The bridge across consisted of two ropes with some old wooden planks suspended between them. It listed back and forth in the breeze.

"I'll tell you what," Laurel said. "If you can cross to the other side without falling off, then we'll treat the entire camp to chocolate cake for dessert tonight."

The campers around me cheered. One girl whispered menacingly, "You better make it across, Holly. I haven't had chocolate in almost a month."

"N-no problem," I stammered. "This will be a cakewalk."

I took a tentative step out onto the bridge's first plank. The wood creaked beneath my feet. The whole bridge swayed under my weight and I instinctively grabbed for the handrail.

I stared out at the task ahead. The first few planks were close enough together, and I stepped carefully from one to the next. I made the mistake once of looking down at the chasm of muddy water below. A wave of dizziness passed over me and from then on, I forced myself to keep my eyes up.

As I traveled across the bridge, the planks became increasingly spaced apart. Around the halfway point, I realized I would have to leap for the next board.

I glanced back the way I came. The campers all watched in anticipation. They seemed to be holding their breaths. "Come on, Holly!" Stella cheered. "I have faith in you—you can do this!"

The longer I waited, the more I was psyching myself out. So I tensed my legs and leaped.

My feet landed on the board successfully. The whole bridge swayed even more than before, threatening to pitch me off into the muck below. I heard the girls all gasp as I tottered on my feet.

Then I regained my balance to the triumphant cries of the campers behind me.

"Just three more planks to go!" one of the other girls shouted.

"You are all that stands between us and cake!" another chimed in.

With my confidence boosted, I completed the next two jumps without a problem. The final one would pose the greatest challenge of all. If I could clear the distance, then the safety of solid ground would just be steps beyond.

I drew in a last deep breath.

Then I propelled myself toward the final plank.

As I sailed through the air, I realized I was going to make it. A triumphant grin spread across my face as my right foot came down on the board.

Then I felt the rotten wooden plank crack in half beneath me. My stomach lurched as I plummeted into the sinkhole below.

For the second time in one day, I helplessly

tumbled into swamp water—only this time from a drop of twenty feet. I plunged into the muddy water so hard that it knocked the wind out of me.

I drew in a relieved gasp as I returned to the surface. To any of the campers staring down into the chasm, I must have looked like a fool, floundering around with my face coated in mud.

But I had far greater problems to worry about.

As I paddled to keep afloat, looking for a way out of the chasm, a dark lump surfaced from the muck just in front of me. Then another one emerged beside it.

At first, I thought they were logs.

Then I saw the green, reptilian eyes.

The leathery snouts.

The rows of sharp teeth.

The two alligators fixed their hungry eyes on me —and they began to swim my way.

A low moan escaped my mouth as the two alligators sliced through the water toward me. I floundered back to the edge of the sinkhole until my back was right up against its muddy sides.

Meanwhile, the gators got close enough that I could see the dark slits of their pupils. Their tails thrashed behind them.

I tried to claw my way up the walls, but there were no handholds to grab onto and the surface was too steep. "Help me!" I screamed. "Somebody throw down a rope!"

But no help came. I turned to face the two gators as they loomed up in front of me, teeth bared and ready to bite into my flesh.

The one nearest me rose right out of the water as it lunged.

I screamed one last time as its gaping jaws aimed for my neck.

Right before the gator could bite me, it abruptly stopped midair, hovering just in front of my face.

And as I stared down its throat, I saw something unexpected:

A human face.

Tonya's face to be exact. The counselor wore swimming goggles and a snorkel, which she spit out of her mouth to grin at me. "Gotcha!" she shouted.

That's when I realized the gator wasn't alive at all —just another prop worn to scare me. The lifelike gator skin was strapped to Tonya's back. The other gator revealed herself to be Heather, a third counselor I'd seen at last night's campfire.

I had been fooled again for the second time in twenty-four hours.

I wondered how long they had been lurking down here in the water, breathing through snorkels and biding their time until I fell in.

I found out later that it was no coincidence that the plank above me had broken. The counselors had rigged a few of the steps to ensure that I fell into the sinkhole so they could give me a good scare. I was lucky to have made it as far across as I did.

Up on the sinkhole's rim, half of the camp gawked down at me. It was official: for the next six weeks, I would always be known as the girl who fell for every scare.

I felt grateful when Stella appeared at the rim and threw down a rope. I climbed it fast, desperate to get away from the laughter. Stella helped pull me out of the sinkhole when I neared the top and she threw a towel around my shoulders. "Don't let those jerks get to you," she told me. "Eventually they'll move on to a new target."

Somehow I doubted that. As long as I continued to prove easy to scare, I might as well have painted a bulls-eye on my back.

THROUGHOUT THE EVENING CAMPFIRE, I kept my guard up. Laurel took the stage to tell another scary story—this time, the tale of a legendary pirate whose vengeful spirit haunted the bayou. My head swiveled as she spoke, expecting a counselor to pop out of the woods to frighten me.

To my great relief, no such attack occurred.

That night, I struggled once again to fall asleep. It could have just been that it was a strange new bed in a sweltering cabin.

It didn't help that the mattress was so lumpy. There was one hard patch right in the middle of my back that I couldn't seem to flatten out, no matter how much I tried.

With a growl of aggravation, I rolled aside and pulled back the sheets to find out what was stabbing me in the back.

That's when I saw the hole in the mattress.

Stuffing spilled out of a long gash in the dingy yellow fabric. It didn't surprise me—everything else around here was falling apart.

The lump that had been annoying me just happened to be underneath the hole. Part of me wanted to find out what was inside the mattress, but I hesitated. There could be bugs living in the bed for all I knew.

However, I decided that I would do just about anything for a good night's sleep. So I slipped my hand into the mattress.

Immediately, my fingertips struck something hard and flat. It took a little jostling, but I was able to pull it free from the mattress.

It was a small wooden box, the size of a book.

On the lid, someone had scrawled three words in jagged writing:

BEWARE THE ROUGAROU

I ran my fingertips over the top of the box. *Beware the Rougarou?* I thought. Wasn't that the werewolf from Laurel's campfire story? The one that prowled the bayou at night?

I looked around the bunk to see if digging in the mattress had woken my roommates. On cue, Stella released a loud snore, so I decided I was safe.

I cautiously opened the lid, half-expecting something to pop out. Instead, I found a pile of dried up flower petals. They looked like they had been red once, but without water, they had shriveled and browned.

I sifted through the flowers and found more items buried inside. There was a video camera, fairly new, but when I clicked on the Power button, nothing happened. The battery must have died.

The box also contained a piece of paper. From the jagged edge, I could tell the page had been torn out of a book.

It was an entry titled "A Brief History of the Rougarou in Southern Louisiana."

I scanned the page. A lot of the information repeated what Laurel had said about them—until I reached the end. Whoever had ripped out the page had circled a few key paragraphs.

Strengths:

Rougarous have an extraordinary sense of smell that helps them track the scent of their prey. Contrary to popular legend, Rougarous don't need the moon to transform into their wolf form and can do so on command at any time. However, they are strongest when the moon is full and bright.

Most Rougarous will attack humans out of hunger. However, the venom in the bite of the Rougarou can transform a human into one of their own. The Rougarou will forever control those they infect with their bite.

Weaknesses:

Like other members of the werewolf family, the Rougarou can be harmed by silver, which acts like a poison in its veins. While many werewolf hunters favor silver bullets, any dagger or other weapon coated in pure silver will suffice.

The Rougarou has also developed a unique allergy to the red spider lily, a plant native to the wetlands. Exposure to the flowers will cause the Rougarou to become sick and temporarily revert back to human form.

I picked up a handful of the dried flowers from the box—these long petals must be spider lilies. If Rachel, the girl who'd vanished, had been the one to hide this, she must have believed in the Rougarou enough that she'd collected these flowers to keep it away.

I turned back to the page. There was one more section highlighted at the bottom.

Warning:

The most dangerous time of year to encounter a Rougarou is the Blood Howl Moon—the first full moon that follows the summer solstice. As the date approaches, the Rougarou grows ever more powerful—and hungrier. Fueled by an appetite they cannot sate, Rougarous have been known to wipe out the population of entire villages in a single night. Even Rougarous that have learned to suppress their animal instincts and live peacefully most of the year cannot fight their blood-thirst as the Blood Howl Moon approaches.

If you cross paths with a Rougarou during this time …

… Then it may already be too late.

Well, that's a little dramatic, I thought.

I discovered one final item in the box I hadn't noticed at first. It was a hand-drawn map of the camp and the surrounding bayou.

A structure at the edge of camp had been crossed out with angry red brushstrokes.

Cabin X, I realized.

I gently closed the lid. My brain swirled with a million thoughts, but two things were immediately clear:

1. The girl who used to sleep in this bunk had taken great care to hide this box from someone—or something.
2. And shortly afterward, without a word, she had disappeared.

13

When I woke up the following morning, my brain still buzzed with questions. What happened to Rachel? What had she filmed with the camera? And why was she so fixated on a mythical wolf beast that couldn't possibly be real?

According to the map she'd left, Cabin X had something to do with all of it. As much as I didn't want to traipse around that creepy abandoned bunk, there might be evidence there that would lead me closer to the truth.

I would have to pay Cabin X a visit.

I bided my time until the afternoon, when I was scheduled for "swim time." After changing into my swimsuit, I waded out into the bayou with a group of other campers. The feel of the weird, spongy ground beneath my toes still made my skin crawl.

One of the other girls smiled at me reassuringly. "It's not so bad once you're in it," she said as she floated by. "The good news is that the more of you that's underwater, the less of your skin is exposed for bugs to bite."

"Thanks," I muttered. Sure enough, a cloud of mosquitos descended on me, so I plunged deeper into the water to escape them.

There was no real structure to swimming time. Some girls played with inner tubes or foam noodles. Some of them were trying to use reeds growing out of the water as snorkels.

I glanced over at Heather, the counselor on lifeguard duty. She wasn't paying attention at all. Instead, her head was practically glued to a handheld video game as she lounged in the tall lifeguard chair.

I decided to make a break for it. I submerged myself up to my neck and paddled out of the designated swimming zone. A few minutes later, the "beach" disappeared from view.

Eventually, I climbed out of the water and tiptoed through camp. Anyone not swimming had gone on a field trip out into the bayou, so it was eerily quiet. Even the frogs had stopped croaking for once.

Cabin X looked just as ominous as I remembered. With its scorched walls and broken windows, I couldn't imagine what sort of tragedy happened there.

I took a deep breath and opened the front door. It creaked on its warped hinges as I cautiously stepped inside.

Rubble littered the floor of Cabin X, thick as a carpet. The walls were charred black as night. The two bunk beds, which probably once resembled the ones in our cabin, now lay on their sides, reduced to smithereens.

Something glinted in the mountain of rubble and I bent to pick it up. It was a jar with a metal lid. I rubbed ash off the glass until I revealed what was inside.

It contained a tuft of gray fur.

"What on earth …" I wondered out loud.

As I sifted through the ashes, I found more odd objects:

Several melted candles.

A long white tooth from an animal.

And a clay bowl stained red with a crusty substance that looked suspiciously like dried blood.

What had happened here? Some kind of bizarre ritual, like the stories claimed?

I was still trying to make sense of the objects I'd found when I heard the crunch of footsteps approach outside.

Someone was heading straight for Cabin X.

I scampered across the floor and hid behind one of the broken beds. If one of the counselors was doing rounds, I'm pretty sure they'd have questions about why I skipped swimming to snoop around someplace off-limits.

I knew something was wrong the moment the door opened. Heavy footsteps lumbered into the cabin, the floorboards straining under their weight. It certainly didn't sound like Laurel in her tennis shoes. No, these belonged to something much larger.

Through the open door, the sunlight cast a rough shadow of someone—or something—on the wall next to me. It walked on two legs like a human, but the shape was all wrong.

Too tall.

Too muscular.

And from what I could tell from the shadow's jagged edges …

Too hairy.

I pressed my back into the ruined mattress, praying it couldn't hear me. The giant creature chewed loudly on something. The food had a fleshy, meaty sound, as though it were gnawing on a turkey leg. Eventually, I heard teeth strike solid bone, and it dropped what it was holding to the ground.

A low, animal grumble escaped its throat.

Then it threw back its head and unleashed a deafening howl.

Staring in horror at its shadow, I saw the long wolf-like snout protruding from its face.

I clamped my hands over my ears to block out the sound.

Just when I thought I was a goner, the creature stopped howling.

Then it loped out of Cabin X, crashing through the exit and disappearing out into the bayou as suddenly as it had arrived.

I stayed behind the mattress for several minutes, until I felt sure it wasn't coming back.

When I finally emerged from my hiding spot, I discovered the monster's abandoned meal. It lay in a bloody pile of bones on top of the rubble. Only a tuft of black and white fur remained on its tail.

The beast had torn a raccoon to shreds.

"You have to believe me!" I cried.

Laurel stood beside me outside Cabin X. After my encounter with the wolf, I had raced back to camp and pleaded with her to follow me. Along the way, I told her about my terrifying encounter with the beast.

Only when we got to Cabin X, the raccoon carcass was gone. Someone had even kicked dirt over the blood.

It was as if it had never even happened.

"It was … it was right here …" I stuttered. "Maybe the wolf came back to finish the rest of its meal and—"

"Holly," Laurel cut me off, crossing her arms. "If I knew that our little campfire prank was going to scare you into seeing things, I would have chosen another victim. The Rougarou is just a local legend—nothing more."

I couldn't seem to find the words. I *knew* what I'd seen, what I'd heard. That ghostly howl, the shadow of the snout, the dead raccoon.

Unless this had all been another elaborate prank, a creature lurked out in the bayou …

Laurel's words were enough to make me second-guess myself. She must have seen my uncertainty, because her face softened. She placed a hand on my shoulder. "Look," she said. "The bayou is a weird place. It takes some adjusting to be this immersed in Mother Nature."

As she guided me back toward camp, she added, "You know what I bet would make you feel better? Tonya is running a letter-writing session in the cafeteria. Why don't you sit down the other campers and write a message home to your father."

As she said that, I realized that this was the longest I'd ever gone without talking to Dad. Without a cell phone, I felt completely disconnected from him —and from the outside world.

So a little while later, I sat down with a group of other campers in the mess hall, where we were given paper and pens.

I wanted so badly to tell him about everything happening here—the missing camper I'd replaced, the crawfish I'd been forced to catch, the counselor's fixation with scaring us.

The werewolf that might be on the loose.

But then I started to feel ungrateful again. My dad had been so proud to send me here. Maybe I was just letting the bayou spook me. Maybe my encounter in Cabin X had a completely rational explanation.

Maybe.

So in the end, I wrote a cheery note telling him how I was having the best summer ever. I filled out the envelope and handed it to Tonya.

As she took it, her eyes burned into mine. "I hope you told him what a blast you're having here," she said.

Her cold, threatening tone made me uneasy. "Of course," I stammered. "Camp Moonglow is everything I ever dreamed of."

I was halfway back to my bunk when I realized I'd written the wrong address on the envelope. Dad and I had moved to a new apartment a few months ago and I still sometimes wrote our old street out of habit. Now I had to go back and fix it.

The cafeteria was dark by the time I returned. Tonya must have left with all of the letters. I remembered seeing a mailbox at the edge of camp, near the counselors' cabin and the director's office. If I hurried, I could catch her before she mailed them.

But when I reached the edge of camp and opened the mailbox, there was nothing inside. It was hard to imagine a postal truck driving all the way out here. Maybe Tonya had to drive to the nearest town to mail them.

I was about to give up when I noticed a flickering light coming from beyond the counselors' cabin. Strange, I thought. Why would someone build a campfire over here when the nightly bonfire would soon begin on the other side of camp?

I edged quietly toward the light. When I turned the corner, I saw Laurel and the other two counselors. A fire burned inside the metal barrel they were standing around.

They didn't see me standing in the shadows. My instincts told me to remain silent and observe them, so I ducked behind the nearest bush.

The counselors were each holding a handful of letters.

The ones the campers and I had just written.

They were reading our mail.

"Listen to this one that Cindy in Cabin Three wrote," Tonya said excitedly. "*I miss you sooooooo much,*

Mommy. How am I supposed to sleep without my stuffed animals here?"

The three of them cackled. "Wait, how about this one?" Heather added. *"The other day I woke up and I realized I'd wet the bed. I had to hide my sheets before my bunkmates saw."*

Tonya high-fived Heather. "She has no idea we've been sneaking in and pouring water on her in the middle of the night."

Laurel's grin dissolved into a scowl as she read the next one. *"I keep hearing the wolf howl at night. The counselors told me it's just a local dog. But one night as I walked to the outhouse, I saw a large figure prowling the edge of the woods. I don't think it's safe here."*

This time none of them laughed. "That's the third camper who's mentioned the Rougarou this week," Heather replied seriously. "We can't have that."

"No, we can't," Laurel agreed. "We can't have that at all."

Then, in unison, the three of them all tossed the letters into the crackling fire.

15

I gasped as the crackling flames consumed the letter I'd just written, along with those from all the other campers.

Even more terrifying: the grins that returned to the counselors' faces as they gleefully watched the letters burn. Laurel looked diabolical as the firelight danced in her eyes.

Something was very wrong here.

Heather cleared her throat. "Even if we keep them from writing home about it, how are we supposed to stop them from talking amongst themselves?" she asked. "When I snoop around the bunks at night, I hear whispers. Girls asking about the wolves, asking where Rachel went."

Laurel stared pensively into the flames. Then she

shrugged. "Let them," she said finally. "In just one night's time, the Blood Howl Moon will rise. In just one night's time, it won't matter."

"I'm just so hungry," Heather complained, her voice whiny. "Can't we snack on a few of the campers tonight?"

"And risk scaring the rest of our prey away?" Laurel snapped. "You can wait another twenty-four hours like the rest of us." She rubbed her hands together. "Then we will feast on an all-you-can-eat buffet."

My blood ran cold. Laurel's final words made me shudder with such force that I lost my balance in the bush where I was hiding. I caught myself before I could topple over completely—but I stepped on a dry twig in the process.

It snapped loudly beneath my feet.

I ducked down and clamped a hand over my mouth. Through the bush, I could see Laurel's head twist in my direction. I held my breath, terrified to make so much as a whisper.

Laurel squinted suspiciously. For a tense moment, I thought her eyes zeroed in on my own.

I let out a relieved breath as she turned back to the fire. She must not have seen me in the shadows.

"Come," Laurel beckoned the others. "We should

prepare for tonight's campfire, then get some rest. Tomorrow is going to be *very* special."

I watched as the three of them strutted off toward the main camp. I held my breath until they disappeared out of sight.

In that moment, I accepted my terrifying new reality:

There wasn't just one werewolf loose in the bayou.

There were *three* of them.

And they were running Camp Moonglow.

16

I slid down against the side of the cabin, overwhelmed with despair. What was I going to do? I wanted to rush back and tell my bunkmates that we were in grave danger.

Would they even listen to me, though? The entire camp probably thought of me as a scaredy-cat. I'd let the counselors terrify me repeatedly in front of everyone. Who would possibly believe my story that Rougarous were real—and they were preparing to eat us?

I also knew that if I went to the police or even my father, they'd never believe me either. No, I would need hard evidence if I had any chance of convincing them.

The secret must lie on the digital camera that

Rachel had left behind. Why else would she have hidden it in the mattress with the other items?

The problem: I still didn't have a way to recharge the camera. Our cabins all had lights, but no electrical outlets. I hadn't seen any in the kitchen either—they cooked everything over fire.

Then I remembered seeing Heather playing that handheld video game. The counselors must have a way to juice up their devices. I would bet anything that they had plugs in their cabin or the director's office.

So I made up my mind: Tonight I was going to sneak back to the other side of camp.

I would make an emergency call from the landline phone in the director's office.

And when I'd charged the camera, I'd have proof once and for all the dark secret that had caused Rachel to go missing—

Before it got the rest of us killed, too.

MY FIRST STEP: I needed something to defend myself against the Rougarous. If they caught me sneaking around the director's cabin, I would be dead meat.

I remembered the encyclopedia entry that Rachel

had left in her secret stash. It claimed that Rougarous were vulnerable to silver weapons.

Unfortunately, that didn't do me much good. It's not like the camp had any swords or silver bullets lying around. They made us eat with plastic utensils in the dining hall, so I couldn't even steal a silver fork if I wanted to.

However, the entry mentioned that Rougarous had a second weakness: spider lilies. I didn't have time to go wandering around the bayou, searching for flowers, so I filled a bag with the dried petals Rachel left in her box. I only hoped they weren't too old to be effective.

My "perfect plan" almost immediately ran into trouble. I had plotted to sneak over to the counselor's cabins during the nightly campfire. With so many campers gathered in one spot, it would be unlikely that Laurel or the others would notice me missing.

Mother Nature had other plans. Close to nightfall, a storm rolled in across camp. As the rain started to come down, Laurel came around to the bunks and announced that the campfire would be canceled. Instead, we would be confined to our bunks for "quiet reading" until curfew.

So I bided my time. I played cards with Darcy, Stella, and Camille while the rain pattered against the roof above us. Eventually, everyone began to yawn and climbed beneath the covers. I pretended to sleep, too, but once I heard the gentle snores of my bunkmates, I slipped quietly out of bed.

I stuffed the camera and its charging cord into my knapsack and quietly opened the screen door. As I stood in the doorway, I cast one last look back at my bunkmates. "I'm going to get help," I promised them in a whisper.

The rain outside came down in sheets. It soaked my clothes within seconds of stepping off the cabin's porch. At least my backpack was waterproof.

I hurried across the dark camp until I reached the rickety porch in front of the director's office. It was so old that the rain dripped through holes in the shingles above.

I pressed my ear to the door, listening for anyone who might be inside. Except for the drizzle pattering against the roof, I heard only silence. Where had the camp director been all this time? And why had nobody thought it suspicious that he'd left three teenagers alone to run an entire camp?

I tried the door handle. Locked.

That didn't change the fact that I needed to get inside the office. I would have to break in through a window.

I circled the cabin, searching for a rock to smash through the glass. Fortunately for me, I discovered that one of the windows in the back had been left ajar. With a hard tug, I lifted it wide enough for me to slip through.

The director's office was dark, except for the light filtering through the windows, so it took a moment for my eyes to adjust. The room wasn't much bigger than our bunks. A large wooden desk took up most of the room. On the cot in the corner, the sheets and pillow showed no signs that anyone had recently slept in them.

Bookshelves lined the walls. I wondered if Camille sneaked here to gather her endless supply of books.

Then I spotted the most important object:

The telephone.

It was one of those old rotary phones, where you had to turn the dial with your finger to make a call. In that moment, I didn't care about having proof. I would call the police and I would make up a reason for them to drive out here to save us.

I picked up the phone and fumbled with the dial as I called 9-1-1. Then I held the receiver to my ear and waited for the voice on the other end to promise me they were coming.

Only I didn't hear anything at all.

No ringing.

No dial tone.

Just dead silence.

Panicked, I grasped the cord at the base of the telephone. I followed it across the room.

When I finally reached the wall by the phone jack, I held up the end of a severed cord. The wires stuck out where someone had cut it.

And in the wall where the phone line used to go were five deep claw marks.

Laurel must have *really* wanted to make sure no one would communicate with the outside world.

I tried not to panic. It was time for Plan B: I would charge the camera and show Darcy, Stella, and Camille to make them believe me. Maybe together, the four of us could escape and get help.

I plugged the camera into the wall outlet by the window. I feared the counselors had killed the electricity, too, but a red light on the digital camera blinked on, indicating that it was charging.

My relief was short-lived. As the storm outside let up, the patter of raindrops was replaced by a more ominous sound:

The whir of an engine.

I peered out through the window in time to see a light drifting through the bayou. As the whirring sound grew louder, I recognized what I was seeing: the headlights on the front of the fanboat, returning to camp.

The boat coasted into the dock and the three counselors jumped onto shore. Laurel supervised the other two as they heaved a big metal trough off the boat. The red creatures inside squirmed and writhed over each other.

At least I finally knew who was eating all the crawfish we'd been catching out in the bayou.

They hung the metal vat over a circle of stones— a fire pit. Laurel placed several logs beneath it and doused them with lighter fluid. She cast a match down into the pit and flames erupted from below.

In that moment, the clouds overhead parted. The nearly full moon gleamed bright against the dark sky, shining down on the three counselors like a spotlight.

I watched as their bodies began to tremble.

Their bones stretched and their muscles thickened until their clothes ripped at the seams. They grew to be six feet, seven feet, eight feet tall.

Brown fur sprouted from their skin.

Snouts extended from their faces, and their lips curled back to reveal gleaming white teeth.

When the transformation was over, three were-wolves stood in the clearing before me.

And as one, they tilted their heads back and let loose a bloodcurdling howl.

18

This can't be happening, I thought. It was one thing to hear the counselors *talk* about being werewolves; it was another thing entirely to see the beasts standing in front of me in the flesh.

Now I was trapped in the director's office. I needed to escape, but if they heard the door open, then the crawfish would only be an appetizer—

And their main course would be Holly, cooked extra rare.

Still, I couldn't look away as the wolf version of Heather reached a claw down into the vat of crawfish. She plucked out one of the little lobsters by its tail. It writhed as she raised it to her gaping jaws. "Time to feast, little one," she rasped.

Before Heather could bite its head off, Laurel swatted her hand. "How many times do I have to tell you," she barked. "You have to cook the crawfish first. It doesn't taste better raw like a human does."

Tonya smirked. "Yeah, Heather, what do you think we are—*animals*?"

Heather started to laugh, but Laurel shoved her toward the director's office. "Don't just stand there. It's your turn to get the spices for the broth."

Heather scratched her hairy head. "Can you, uh, remind me which spices those are again?"

Laurel let loose a growl of exasperation. "Black peppercorns, coriander, paprika, and cayenne pepper."

"Yes, cayenne pepper," Tonya echoed, rubbing her hands together. "You didn't make the broth spicy enough last time."

Heather grumbled in response.

Then she trudged toward the cabin where I was hiding.

Dread flooded me once again. There wasn't exactly an abundance of hiding spots in the office.

In my terror, an idea came to me. It was a long shot, but it might be my one chance to put these evil werewolves out of commission.

I stumbled over to the shelf where they stored all the spices and looked through them until I found the one labeled "Cayenne pepper." I opened it and dumped the red powder into the trash.

In my pocket, I found the sack of spider lily petals. I ground up the dried flowers between my palms until they turned powdery, then funneled them into the pepper container.

As I screwed the lid closed, the office doorknob rattled. Heather cursed and her keys jingled as she looked for the right one to unlock it.

With only seconds to spare, I put the spice back on the shelf and lunged across the room. Just as I rolled beneath the cot, the office door flew open.

I cowered in my hiding spot, pressed flat against the floor. The bedsheet would help conceal me, but if Heather stopped to look here, I was doomed.

The floorboards creaked ominously under her heavy footsteps. I held my breath as her fur-covered feet lumbered past the bed, her sharp nails gouging scratches into the floor with each step.

I heard her muttering on the other side of the room as she plucked various spices from the shelves. "Coriander, paprika ... Ah, here's the cayenne pepper," she said.

On her way out, her shadow once again fell over the bed.

Only this time, she paused.

I heard the *sniff, sniff, sniff* as her nose tested the air—

Followed by a low growl as she smelled the scent of the human hiding nearby.

19

My heart hammered in my chest. This was it. Heather would bend down, lift the sheet, and find me hiding beneath the bed.

When the counselors ate me, they wouldn't even bother to cook me first.

Then a miracle happened. "Heather!" Laurel's voice boomed from outside. "What is taking you so long? Some of us would like to eat before sunrise."

Above me, Heather grumbled. "Someday I'll be the boss around here," she vowed under her breath.

With that, she stormed out of the office and slammed the door behind her.

I finally allowed myself to breathe again. Once I felt confident she wasn't coming back, I crawled out from beneath the bed and over to the window.

I peered over the sill as Heather joined the other two wolves by the crawfish pot. Without bothering to measure out the spices, she dumped them all one by one into the boiling water.

I watched in suspense as she unscrewed the cayenne pepper bottle and sprinkled the lily petals into the pot.

They let the crawfish boil for a few minutes. By then, even Laurel had grown hungry and impatient. "Enough of this," she growled and kicked the pot off its perch. It landed on its side, spilling its contents over the muddy soil.

Tonya and Heather both yelped and leaped back as the hot water nearly scorched their fur. As the water seeped into the soil, a mountain of bright red crawfish remained.

The three wolves dropped to their haunches. They didn't even bother to use their claws—they just buried their snouts in the pile of crawfish. Their knife-sharp teeth ripped the shells apart so they could devour the soft juicy flesh within.

My heart sank as they feasted. The spider lilies hadn't even slowed them down. I should have known better than to trust a book page I found stuffed in a mattress.

Then Tonya suddenly straightened up. She

pressed her clawed fingers to her stomach. A loud belch echoed from her mouth. "I … I don't feel so good," she stammered.

The other two began to look sickly as well. Laurel doubled over and coughed as though she were hacking up a hairball. "Heather, how much pepper did you put in this?" she moaned between retches.

Eventually, the three of them toppled onto their sides, clutching their stomachs. As the spider lily poison set in, their bodies contracted back to their original size. The fur returned to the pale skin it had grown from.

When it was all over, the counselors looked as human as they'd ever been. They continued to roll around in their shredded, stretched out uniforms.

Inside the office, I pumped my fist in triumph. Hopefully, the lily poison would keep them out of wolf form long enough to convince the other campers to leave with me.

Fortunately, I had evidence now. I snatched the camera, which had finally recharged enough to turn on. I raced back to my bunk to show Darcy, Stella, and Camille. Once they believed me, it would be much easier to persuade the other campers.

I threw open the door to Cabin IX. My three bunkmates woke with a start. I must have looked crazed standing in the doorway, backlit by the moonlight.

"Holly?" Darcy muttered sleepily. She glanced at the clock. "What time is it?"

Stella rubbed her eyes. "And why do you look like you were chased by a wild animal?"

"I need to show you something," I said urgently. "Please, I wouldn't wake you in the middle of the night if it wasn't an emergency."

To their credit, Camille, Darcy, and Stella slipped out of bed. They knelt around me as I powered on the camera.

"I know this sounds crazy, but the counselors running the camp aren't who they say they are," I explained. "They're monsters, and they're planning to eat us all tomorrow night."

My bunkmates exchanged glances that clearly said, *Well, our friend has finally lost it.* "Holly ..." Camille started to say.

I cut her off. "I'm going to show you proof. After that, if you still don't believe me, then you're welcome to go back to bed. But this situation is life or death."

My urgency must have gotten through to them because Darcy nodded. "Let's see it then," she said.

With my three friends crowded behind me, I pressed play.

The video began with the lens facing directly at a girl about my age—Rachel, I assumed. She was pale with long black hair. Behind her, the bayou's cypress trees were steeped in shadow.

She stared gravely into the camera. "She's been sneaking off to Cabin X every night for the last week," Rachel explained in a whisper. "No one here believes me when I tell them she's up to something bad, so tonight I'm going to prove the truth once and for all:

"That this girl is pure evil."

The image cut to a shot of her approaching one of the bunks. It was Cabin X, but not the charred ruin as we knew it now. Back then, the bunk resembled all the others, with no trace of the fire that had destroyed it.

Rachel pointed the camera lens through one of the open windows. Inside the cabin, a girl sat at a small wooden table covered in candles. Their flames cast an eerie orange glow over the room.

The girl had her back to the camera, so it was impossible to make out her face. However, her voice sounded oddly familiar as she started to speak. "From the great powers beyond, I summon the great Rougarou," she intoned. She lifted a bowl over her head. "I present you with the sacrificial gifts you requested: the hair of a wolf, the tooth of an alligator ... and my own blood."

In response, the sky above rumbled with thunder. The girl rose slowly out of her chair and tilted her face toward the ceiling. "Once I say the sacred words, I call on you to fill me with the powers of the Rougarou to vanquish my enemies," she shouted. "*LUPUS ... ULULATE ... SANGUINEM ... LUNA!*"

After she uttered the strange words, the rumble of thunder abruptly stopped.

Then a lightning bolt pierced down through the roof.

The electrical charge punched a hole through the ceiling with a mighty bang. A blinding light filled the room. To Rachel's credit, she managed to hold the camera steady.

The lightning bolt struck the girl at the table. Her body vibrated as the energy passed through her. I gasped as I watched, thinking for sure she would die of electrocution.

But then the lightning vanished as quickly as it had forked down. The girl miraculously remained standing. For a minute or so, she wobbled on her feet, as smoke rose off her scorched clothing.

Eventually, I heard the sounds of other girls laughing as they approached Cabin X. The front door popped open, and I recognized the three girls that walked through.

Laurel.

Tonya.

Heather.

They stopped laughing as soon as they saw the girl standing in front of them at her ceremonial table.

"What are you doing here, you pipsqueak?" Tonya snapped. "This is *our* bunk."

Laurel was the first to notice the gaping hole in the ceiling. The edges still glowed with embers from the lightning strike. "And what did you do to our roof?" she cried.

The three of them advanced on the intruder—but they stopped dead in their tracks.

The girl's body began to stretch taller. Behind me, Darcy whispered "What on Earth ...?" as the camper on screen transformed into the Rougarou before our very eyes.

"T-this can't be real," Stella stuttered in disbelief.

In the video, the three counselors were also struggling to believe what they were seeing. The werewolf lunged for Laurel first. She bit the counselor on the arm, and then quickly pounced on the other two as they tried to escape.

In the process, she knocked over the table covered in candles. Fire erupted on the floor.

After she'd bitten each of them, the Rougarou slowly returned to her human form. She stood over the three counselors, who pleaded with the girl to let them live, while Cabin X burned around them.

"Oh, you'll live," the girl said. "Now that you've been bitten by me, you have no choice but to serve me. I am your master, your Alpha Dog, and you will do as I say from this day forward."

Realization dawned on me as I watched. I might have poisoned three Rougarous back at the counselor's cabin.

But the master who made them was still out there in the bayou.

As the video zoomed in on the girl, she snapped her head around to face the camera. We heard Rachel gasp, and then the camera fell to the ground before it shut off completely. The video ended in static.

All it took was a fraction of a second for us to see the face of the girl who'd turned herself into a werewolf.

It was Camille.

Darcy, Stella, and I slowly turned around to look at our fourth bunkmate.

Camille was locking the cabin door. "I really wish the three of you hadn't seen that ..." she whispered somberly.

21

I couldn't believe it. All this time, the leader of the Rougarou pack had been living right under our own roof.

Now she stood between the three of us and the cabin's exit.

"I … I don't understand," I told her. "You *chose* to become a werewolf?"

Camille crossed her arms and leaned against the doorframe. "I've been coming here every summer since I was seven, and it was always the same—the older girls scaring the younger ones they saw as weaker." The corners of her lips turned up in a wicked smile. "So I decided to become something that could scare *them*."

Stella giggled nervously. "Well, it sure worked. You are definitely the scariest person in camp."

"Thank you," Camille replied proudly. "None of the other campers—not even you, my own bunkmates—suspected how powerful I was. Bookworm by day, bloodthirsty huntress by night. You all slept so soundly you never heard me slip out at night to prowl the bayou for prey."

"But Rachel noticed," I replied.

"Yes," Camille agreed. Her eyes narrowed. "And that's why she had to go."

Darcy whimpered. "How could you do that to her?" she asked, tears running down her face. "She was our friend."

Camille shrugged. "Rachel learned the truth and threatened to tell everyone," she replied. "I couldn't have her scaring away my livestock."

"Livestock?" I repeated.

Then I realized with a shudder that she was talking about *us*.

"As a Rougarou, I was more powerful than I ever imagined," Camille continued, pacing in front of the door. "But I never predicted how hungry I would be. Some days scavenging for animals in the bayou is enough to sustain me. However, as the Blood Howl Moon grows nearer, the hunger pains become unbearable. So I thought to myself: where could I find enough meat to feed myself and my wolf pack? This camp would be the perfect buffet for us. No adults. No one to save you." A line of drool dribbled out of Camille's open mouth. "And forty delicious campers for us to feast upon."

"You don't have to do this," I pleaded with her. "No one has to get eaten tonight."

Camille considered this. "I thought about biting you to make you join my pack. The three of you have always been nice to me." Even as she said it, Camille's body began to stretch taller, and wider, until her head brushed the ceiling and her hulking body filled the doorway. Fur sprouted from her skin and her sharp fangs gleamed white. In Rougarou form, she was even larger than the counselors.

Her next words came out in a raspy growl:

"... But the three of you smell so delicious, I can't help myself."

Without warning, Camille vaulted across the room in a single leap. Darcy and Stella dove one way to avoid her, and I dove the other.

Our werewolf bunkmate collided with the back wall so hard that the window shattered. The whole cabin shook and dust rained down from the ceiling.

The collision only stunned her briefly. With a

snarl, she turned on me. As I backed into the corner, I searched frantically for something to defend myself with. Behind me was Darcy's nightstand, so I opened one of the drawers and grasped around inside.

My fingers found something hard and pointy. I pulled it out, hoping it was a Swiss Army Knife.

I groaned. It was a macaroni art starfish she'd made in crafting class.

Camille threw back her head and howled with laughter. "Oh, please don't hurt me with your dangerous pasta ornament!" she mocked me. "I'm on a low-carb diet!"

She leaned down toward me, jaws parting to take a bite out of my throat.

22

Just when I thought I was wolf chow, two shadows rose up behind Camille.

Stella and Darcy threw a quilt over the wolf's head. Before she knew what was happening, my two bunkmates had wrestled the quilt down over her thick arms and wrapped it around her tightly with a roll of the tape Stella used to design her clothes.

When they were done, Camille tottered around the cabin on two hairy legs. The quilt and tape had trapped her arms against her sides, and her murderous snarls sounded muffled through the blanket.

Stella, out of breath, held up the empty tape roll.

"It's not one of my best fashion designs, but it should hold her for—"

She never got to finish her sentence. One of Camille's claws tore right through the quilt and grabbed Stella around the neck. The wolf hurled our bunkmate across the room. She hit the wall hard and landed dazed in the opposite corner.

Camille ripped the rest of the quilt off of her head and chest. It exploded in a cascade of white feathers.

The wolf advanced on Stella, who was struggling to get to her feet. Her claws glimmered in the moonlight filtering through the window.

Seeing my friend about to be eaten spurred me into action. I dashed over to one of the bunk beds. Darcy seemed to read my mind and joined me.

"Stella, roll out of the way now!" I yelled.

Our friend gathered her wits enough to follow our directions. She scampered out of the corner, just barely dodging a vicious swipe from Camille's claws.

Darcy and I gave the bunk bed a hard push and it toppled right over onto Camille. The bed flattened her to the ground. I hoped that maybe it would knock her out, but even pinned beneath the bed, she hissed, "Your deaths will not be quick!"

The three of us unlocked the door and escaped out into the night air. I knew there was no way the bed would hold her for long.

"You two need to go warn all the others," I instructed them. "Wake them up. Do whatever you can to make them believe. Everyone who doesn't escape this camp is a goner."

"What are you going to do?" Darcy asked.

I stared off in the direction of the ropes course. An idea was forming.

"I'm going to set a wolf trap," I replied finally.

I didn't have a chance to explain any further. A howl erupted from Cabin IX.

Moments later, an object burst through the roof, scattering shingles in all directions. It flew through the air like a missile and clattered across the ground until it landed just in front of our feet.

It was the mangled metal frame of the bunk bed. Camille had crushed it as if it were a soda can.

We didn't need any more convincing. Darcy and Stella sprinted toward the other bunks and I dashed off in the opposite direction.

Right as I risked a glance over my shoulder, the side of our cabin exploded as Camille broke through it.

She lingered in the wolf-shaped hole, seething with anger, her chest puffing in and out.

Then her glowing yellow eyes focused on me.

23

I sprinted through the dark camp as fast as my legs would carry me. I didn't dare look back again, but I could hear the wolf's feet loping over the ground.

It was so dark that I nearly fell into the sinkhole.

I didn't know I'd reached the Slurry pit until I felt my foot step into open air where I expected there to be ground. I tottered on the edge of the dark pit, and it was a miracle I didn't fall right in.

The Slurry gaped before me. In the dark, it was impossible to see the water below. It was as if I fell in the sinkhole I would simply tumble into eternity, all the way to the center of the earth.

I shook off that mental image. Instead, I focused on my plan.

See, I'd realized that Camille was faster than me in her Rougarou form, so I couldn't outrun her.

She had a powerful sense of smell, so I couldn't hide from her.

She had rippling muscles, so I couldn't overpower her.

But maybe, just maybe, I could outsmart her.

The day I'd fallen into the Slurry, Camille hadn't been paying attention. Maybe she didn't know the rope bridge's dark secret: that the counselors had broken some of the boards so campers would fall in.

Well, tonight I was going to use that to my advantage.

I stepped out onto the bridge and began to hop my way across the gaps. Now I could see what I'd missed during my first encounter with the Slurry: the counselors had marked each of the booby-trapped planks with a tiny skull and crossbones. As I crossed, I made sure to skip each of those boards.

I was halfway across when a piercing howl echoed from behind me.

The Rougarou had arrived.

Camille stepped out onto the bridge. Under her weight, the entire bridge wobbled beneath me and I gripped the rails to keep my balance.

She pounced one plank closer to me. "You know,

I initially liked you," she snarled. "I wanted you to be a member of my pack. Wouldn't you love to help me boss around Laurel and the other counselors, after all they did to you?"

I looked down. The plank just in front of me had the "danger" marking on it. I just needed to wait for Camille to get a little bit closer …

I shook my head. "You know, I'm on a very strict 'no human' diet, so I really have no interest in joining your pack."

"Suit yourself," Camille growled. "In my world, if you're not the predator …" She pounced another step closer. "… Then you're the prey."

It took all my courage not to back away as she closed the distance between us. Soon, she was close enough that I could see the saliva glistening on her teeth and smell the meat on her breath. Her eyes glowed yellow in the dark.

"I just want you to know one thing before I eat you." Her fangs glimmered in the moonlight as she grinned. "I won't let one morsel of you go to waste."

Camille took a final step toward me, so close that her fur brushed my face.

Then, with a sharp crack, the plank snapped in half beneath her.

Camille gave a surprised yelp as she fell through the bridge.

I didn't even have a second to celebrate my victory over her—because as Camille fell, she wrapped a claw around my ankle.

24

I screamed as she started to drag me down with her. I tightened my fingers on the handrails, but it was hard to hold on with a werewolf dangling from my foot.

I tried to kick her off of me, but that only made her angrier. Her sharp claws dug into the skin around my ankle. She was going to twist my knee right out of my socket if I didn't get her off soon.

Or worse, I'd fall with her into the Slurry, where there would be no escape.

As I stared down at the terrifying beast, something glinted in my line of vision. It was the locket around my neck, the one with the picture of my mother.

The answer had been within my reach the entire time:

The locket was made of silver.

With her sinewy arms, Camille began to pull herself up using my leg. She bared her teeth, preparing to sink those fangs into my flesh.

If I released my grip on the handrails to take the locket off my neck, I wasn't sure I'd be able to hold on with just one hand. So I bent over as low as I could go. The locket dangled just inches from Camille's snout as her jaws parted to bite me.

With one last effort, I forced myself to bend over just a little farther.

The locket landed on Camille's snout. When the silver made contact, a plume of smoke rose up from her fur. As it began to burn her, she let out a pained yowl.

Unable to bear the agony of the silver any longer, Camille released my ankle. I watched as the giant werewolf flailed and tumbled into the sinkhole.

She hit the water with a mighty splash. When she resurfaced, there was murder in her glowing eyes. "You'll pay for this!" she screamed, rubbing her burned nose. "When I get out of here, I'll make you my personal chew toy."

They were empty threats. I watched in relief as

she struggled and failed to climb out of the sinkhole. She kept trying to jump out, but even with her incredible strength, she would only make it halfway up before she'd fall back in a splash. When she tried to climb out, she just ended up with claws full of mud.

I marveled at the locket around my neck. All those years ago when my dad gave me this, little did he know this picture of my mother would one day save my life.

"Thanks, Mom," I whispered and went to kiss the locket—

Only to discover a tuft of singed werewolf fur stuck to the silver.

I wrinkled my nose and added, "I promise to give you a thorough cleaning later."

25

Of course, most of the other campers didn't believe us at first when we tried to explain why we needed to escape the camp.

However, they changed their tune after we led them over to the Slurry pit. Camille was still in wolf form, and she was angrier than ever. One snap of her enormous jaws and everyone backed away from the sinkhole.

With the help of the other girls, we forced the three counselors to join Camille down in the Slurry. In their weakened state, still poisoned from the spider lilies, they couldn't resist all forty of us.

As we walked away from Camp Moonglow, the first rays of dawn gave the sky a rosy tinge. It gave me hope that everything was going to be okay.

We'd only made it a mile down the road when a girl my age stepped out from behind a tree. In the dim light, it was hard to make out her features at first, but when we got closer, I recognized her:

The long, stringy black hair.

The pale skin and dark circles around her eyes.

Rachel, the missing camper.

"Rachel, you're alive!" Stella cried happily. "We thought for sure that the wolves had eaten you." She and Darcy rushed forward to embrace their lost bunkmate.

Rachel smirked as they hugged her. "Those goons, eat me? Not a chance."

One thing about Rachel's disappearance had been bothering me this whole time. "Rachel, there's something I still don't get," I said. "You discovered that Camille was a Rougarou *last* summer. So why on earth did you come back to camp this year?"

Rachel smiled again. "Oh, that part is simple," she replied. "When I learned that Camille and the counselors were monsters like me, I wanted in on their plan. But the four of them didn't want to share."

We all took a cautious step back. What did she mean by "*monsters like me*?"

I didn't have to wonder for long. Rachel's skin

began to turn green and scaly. Her hair fell out and her face elongated into the leathery snout of a gator. She grew so tall that her head brushed the leaves above her.

The gator monster known as Rachel loomed over us. She ran a long pointy tongue over her rows of killer teeth. "And now that you've gotten rid of the wolves for me …" she growled. "… *I can eat you all to myself.*"

Camp Moonglow was a ghost town. There were no more counselors barking orders, no more campers gossiping in their bunks, no bugle call to summon everyone to dinner.

There was only the croak of bullfrogs in the bayou.

Then a heavy wind picked up from the west. It swept through camp, stirring the dead leaves where they lay on the ground.

A glowing portal opened up in the air, as though someone had sliced it open with a knife. The edges of the portal burned green, and if anyone had been standing there, they would have seen a window into another world:

A sky with multiple moons.

An alien landscape covered in red soil.

The skeleton of a gargantuan creature, and growing inside of it, a field of colorful, monstrous eggs …

And of course, no one would miss the tall man in the white lab coat as he stepped through the portal, into camp. His skin was so eerily pale and smooth it could have been painted on. The wind ruffled his dark beard as the rift in the air sealed shut behind him and the alien world disappeared with it.

Through his dark goggles, Dr. Umbra surveyed the wreckage of Camp Moonglow with a frown. It had only been two weeks since his last visit. How had it come to this?

The doctor wandered through camp, searching for any signs of life. He didn't find any until he got to the rope course. As he approached, the snarls of several creatures echoed from the sinkhole.

Down in the soggy pit, two wolves fought over the carcass of a duck that had been unfortunate enough to land in the water near them. They each sank their teeth into it and were playing a game of tug-of-war.

A third wolf swooped in and stole it right out of their jaws. She swallowed the bird in one bite while the others snarled at her.

Camille remained in human form. She leaned sullenly at the edge of the pit, pouting at the water with her arms tightly folded over her chest.

When Camille saw the man standing on the edge of the sinkhole, her eyes suddenly lit up and she hopped to her feet. "Director Umbra!" she exclaimed. "I knew you'd come to rescue us."

The three counselors abruptly changed back into human form, looking somewhat ashamed at their behavior. With their tattered clothing and dirt-smeared faces, they looked particularly pathetic. Laurel coughed up a mouthful of feathers.

Dr. Umbra lowered his goggles. His tangerine eyes burned with anger. "I left you in charge for one week," he roared, so fiercely that the counselors retreated to the back of the pit. "And this is what I come back to?"

All three started babbling excuses at once, but he cut them off with a sharp slice of his hand. He spoke one word into the intercom on his lapel: "Daughter."

Another portal carved a hole in the air beside him. A woman with vibrantly red hair and the same glowing eyes as Dr. Umbra stepped through the rift. "Yes, father?" she said.

"What's the planet in the Piscium system, the one with the big zoo where they keep humans like animals?" The name was on the tip of his tongue. "Bova, Bloma …"

"Bleaka, father," she replied calmly.

Dr. Umbra snapped his fingers. "That's the one! Send our friends here to the zookeeper there." He stared down into the pit. "Tell him I've got a new werewolf exhibit for him."

"No, wait—!" the four girls started to wail.

The woman typed something into her digital clipboard, and with a final tap, a portal opened up beneath the wolves. They plummeted through it into another dimension, along with a cascade of Slurry water. When the portal sealed shut, it silenced their screams.

Dr. Umbra cast a final look back at the desolate camp and sighed. "This place had so much potential for havoc and mayhem. I need some cheering up— tell me about the most terrifying project you're working on."

"Well, my favorite is a botanical garden that turns all who enter it into an army of plant soldiers …"

The doctor nodded. "Now you're talking," he said. He pointed to the void where Camille and the counselors had been just moments before. "But I can't keep trusting these tasks to amateurs." He placed a hand on her shoulder. "Daughter, I want *you* to handle this one personally."

A wicked grin spread across her face. "It would be my honor, father."

A PREVIEW OF BONEGARDEN #2

THE GODS OF LAVA COVE

I was going to die on this plane.

At least that's what I was convinced. Sure, I had flown in big commercial airliners a few times before when my family went on vacation.

But this was a small pontoon plane, barely larger than my bedroom. I felt like I was hurtling through the sky in a minivan with wings. Except for the pilot, I was the plane's only passenger as it flew over the Pacific Ocean at a hundred miles per hour.

Storm clouds pressed in around us. One of the propellers whirred just outside my porthole window. I imagined it flying off and sheering the whole plane in half.

Before this story takes a dark turn, I should probably spare a moment to tell you a little about myself and how I ended up on this tiny plane—while I'm still alive to tell the tale.

My name is Kalon, and I'm twelve years old. I've spent most of my life growing up in a small town in Maine, where the biggest risk I face on a daily basis is being *bored* to death.

So you can imagine how excited I was when my Aunt Samira, a famous archaeologist, invited me to visit her on the tropical island of Caldera.

It sounded like a dream come true. I'd grown up watching movies about famous adventurers like *Indiana Jones*. Why read about history in a textbook when I could be out living it?

While my teachers in school droned on in class, I daydreamed about exploring a lost pyramid, dodging booby traps until I discovered a tomb filled with treasure. With a priceless artifact clutched in my hands, I'd flee the angry mummy I'd just awakened from centuries of slumber.

I guess you could say I have an overactive imagination.

Over the loud hum of the propellers, the pilot shouted, "There it is!" He pointed out the window.

I pressed my face to the foggy glass and peered out. The island rose dramatically out of the churning ocean. Caldera was known for three things:

The strange purple sands that colored the beach.

The archaeological sites of the ancient people who had settled there two thousand years ago.

And, of course, the fiery volcano.

Even through the rain, I could see the dark cone rising out of the jungle and the plume of smoke drifting out of the crater at the top. Aunt Samira had assured my mom that the volcano was perfectly safe to be around.

I didn't think adults were supposed to lie.

"We'll be landing in just a couple of minutes," the pilot assured me. "I just need to find—"

He never finished his sentence. As I watched through the window, a bolt of lightning lanced out of the storm clouds. In a blinding flash of light, it struck the propeller.

The bang it made was deafening. I couldn't stop myself from shrieking.

I watched in horror as the propeller sputtered and then stopped spinning altogether.

Then the plane started to tilt toward its nose.

We were going down!

2

"Hold on!" the pilot yelled.

In a matter of seconds, we entered a steep nose-dive. The speed of our descent flattened me against the back of my seat. My stomach lurched into my throat. I felt like I was on a roller coaster careening down the tracks—only at the bottom, we wouldn't just harmlessly coast up another hill.

"Come on, come on …" the pilot muttered as he pulled up on the throttle. The plane rattled around us as though it was about to break apart. The ocean below grew closer until I could see only blue out my window.

Just when I was about to give up hope, I heard a heartening sound. The propeller outside coughed, then sputtered back to life. The blades began to spin again, picking up speed until they became invisible to the naked eye.

I exhaled a sigh of relief as the plane leveled out. A few moments later, the pontoons skimmed across the water. The plane coasted over the choppy waves until we slowed to a stop near the beach.

The pilot turned back to look at me, a huge grin under his thick mustache. You'd never know he'd just escaped a near brush with death. "Piece of cake," he said. "My landings are always smooth as butter."

"What kind of butter do you eat?" I blurted out before I could stop myself.

His laughter echoed through the plane.

I couldn't wait to get out of the rickety metal death trap. I heaved open the door.

With shaky legs, I jumped down into the shallow water. It was much warmer than the frigid ocean I was used to back home.

The first thing I noticed about the island was the violet beach—sand as vibrantly purple as grape jelly. The beach transitioned into a dense, green jungle that covered most of the island.

But the feature that really captured my attention was the volcano.

The pilot must have seen me looking up at the smoking crater because he clapped a big hairy hand on my shoulder. "Don't you worry, mate," he said. "Mount Caldera only erupts once every thirty years."

I relaxed a little. "How long ago was the last eruption?" I asked.

"Twenty-nine years and three quarters!" He threw back his head and laughed uproariously.

"Very funny," I replied. The captain had already started walking toward the beach with my suitcase, so I called after him. "You *are* joking, right?"

As I splashed through the water behind him, I spotted a woman standing on the purple sand, waving at me. It had been a few years since I last saw Aunt Samira, but she hadn't changed a bit. She had the same light brown skin as me, and jet black hair pulled into a frizzy bun. She wore a matching khaki shirt and shorts and a wide-brimmed hat that made her look like she'd just completed a safari.

Aunt Samira spread her arms. "Welcome, Kalon," she said. "Welcome to Caldera."

Behind her, the volcano rumbled ominously.

Made in the USA
Coppell, TX
28 December 2019